Dear Parent:

Congratulations! Your child is taking the first steps on an exciting journey. The destination? Independent reading!

STEP INTO READING® will help your child get there. The program offers five steps to reading success. Each step includes fun stories and colorful art. There are also Step into Reading Sticker Books, Step into Reading Math Readers, Step into Reading Write-In Readers, Step into Reading Phonics Readers, and Step into Reading Phonics First Steps! Boxed Sets—a complete literacy program with something for every child.

Learning to Read, Step by Step!

Ready to Read Preschool–Kindergarten
• big type and easy words • rhyme and rhythm • picture clues
For children who know the alphabet and are eager to begin reading.

Reading with Help Preschool–Grade 1
• basic vocabulary • short sentences • simple stories
For children who recognize familiar words and sound out new words with help.

Reading on Your Own Grades 1–3
• engaging characters • easy-to-follow plots • popular topics
For children who are ready to read on their own.

Reading Paragraphs Grades 2–3
• challenging vocabulary • short paragraphs • exciting stories
For newly independent readers who read simple sentences with confidence.

Ready for Chapters Grades 2–4
• chapters • longer paragraphs • full-color art
For children who want to take the plunge into chapter books but still like colorful pictures.

STEP INTO READING® is designed to give every child a successful reading experience. The grade levels are only guides. Children can progress through the steps at their own speed, developing confidence in their reading, no matter what their grade.

Remember, a lifetime love of reading starts with a single step!

To Lulu, our new puppy.
(She's a Westie!)
You're super cute—and you toot!
—J.J.

In loving memory of Dan Pacelli—
father, teacher, and friend
—P.Z.

Special thanks to Katonah and Lewisboro elementary schools

Photography by Sandra Kress

Cleanup and inking by Vinh Troung

Digital coloring and compositing by Paul Zdanowicz

Copyright © 2006 by Sesame Workshop and Cartoon Pizza, Inc. PINKY DINKY DOO and associated characters, trademarks, and design elements are owned and licensed by Cartoon Pizza, Inc., and Sesame Workshop. Sesame Workshop and its logos are trademarks and service marks of Sesame Workshop. All rights reserved under International and Pan-American Copyright Conventions. Published in the United States by Random House Children's Books, a division of Random House, Inc., New York, and simultaneously in Canada by Random House of Canada Limited, Toronto, in conjunction with Sesame Workshop.

www.stepintoreading.com

Educators and librarians, for a variety of teaching tools, visit us at
www.randomhouse.com/teachers

Library of Congress Cataloging-in-Publication Data
Jinkins, Jim.
Pinky Dinky Doo : Pinky Stinky Doo / by Jim Jinkins.
   p.   cm. — (Step into reading. Step 3)
SUMMARY: Pinky Dinky Doo tells her little brother a story about a girl who passes gas in front of her classmates, but instead of revenge for the teasing, she invokes the Golden Rule.
ISBN 0-375-83511-3 (trade) — ISBN 0-375-93511-8 (lib. bdg.)
[1. Flatulence—Fiction. 2. Storytelling—Fiction. 3. Schools—Fiction.
4. Golden rule—Fiction.] I. Title: Pinky Stinky Doo. II. Title.
III. Series: Step into reading. Step 3 book.
PZ7.J57526Pfu 2006 [Fic]—dc22 2005001209

Printed in the United States of America   First Edition   10 9 8 7 6 5 4 3 2 1

STEP INTO READING, RANDOM HOUSE, and the Random House colophon are registered trademarks of Random House, Inc.

Pinky Dinky Doo™

Pinky Stinky Doo

by Jim Jinkins

Random House 🏠 New York

Mr. Guinea Pig

Tyler Doo

Mommy Doo

Daddy Doo

Pinky Dinky Doo

Nicholas Biscuit

Daffinee Toilette

Bobby Boom

Abby McTabby

Lane Puppytray

Ross Applesauce

"Didn't you wear those yesterday?"

Pinky asked.

"Yeah,"

Tyler replied.

"And the day before that,

and the day before that.

I always wear them

because they're lucky!"

6

"My lucky socks stink!"
Tyler shouted.
"I can't wear smelly socks
to school!"
"Why don't we wash them?"
Pinky suggested.
"And while they're drying—"

"Are you going to
make up a story
about super-lucky socks?"
asked Tyler.
"No, little brother,"
Pinky replied,
"this story is going to be about
something super smelly."

"Like what?"
asked Tyler.
"Like about a girl I know
named Pinky Stinky Doo!"
said Pinky.
"Who?"
asked Tyler.

"Listen,"

Pinky said.

"I'll just shut my eyes,

wiggle my ears,

and crank up my imagination."

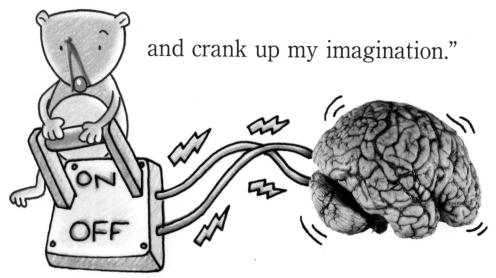

"The name of this story is . . ."

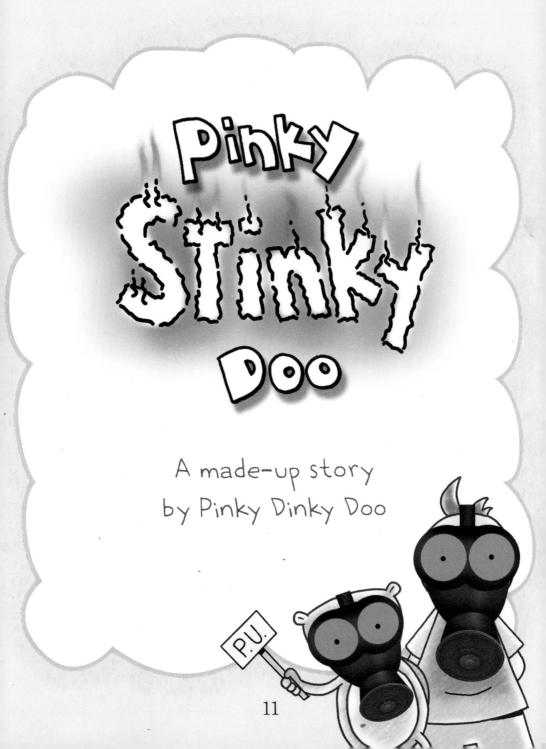

Pinky Stinky Doo

A made-up story
by Pinky Dinky Doo

11

One day in

Great Big City,

Daddy Doo surprised the family
with a very special breakfast.

He made great big
Veggie Wedgie Beanie Weenie
Neato Breakfast Burritos!

The whole family dug in.

Then Pinky was off to school.

13

It was a perfectly normal day.

Everything was going fine—

until lunchtime.

Pinky's tummy began

to rumble and tumble

and feel kind of funny.

Nicholas Biscuit was telling jokes.

Then everybody started to tell
their own favorite funny jokes.

They were all
laughing really hard.

Pinky was laughing like crazy.

Her stomach was really
rocking and rolling.

Then,

all of a sudden—

Toot

Pinky Dinky Doo
accidentally passed
the tiniest little bit of gas.

Pinky hoped
that nobody had noticed.
But . . .

HA   HA   HA

HA   HA   HA

Hey, everybody . . .
guess who tooted!!!

HA   HA   HA

Everyone started laughing
at Pinky Dinky Doo.

Daffinee started chanting.

STINKY PINKY!
STINKY PINKY!

Pinky's friends all repeated
her new name.

Pinky turned very pink.

She wondered if

Stinky Pinky Doo

would be her name forever.

Pinky felt really bad
and really sad.

For dinner that night,
Mommy Doo served
salad and bread.

The whole family
was suffering
from breakfast.
Nobody was very hungry.
Not even Mr. Guinea Pig.

"Those Veggie Wedgie
Beanie Weenie
Neato Breakfast Burritos
made me toot today!"
cried Pinky.
"And everyone made fun of me!"
Pinky was pretty mad.

25

Daddy Doo gave Pinky a few helpful suggestions:

"Why don't you . . .

A Move your friends to Stinktopia and become queen?

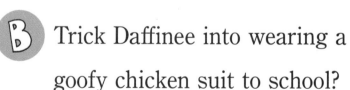

B Trick Daffinee into wearing a goofy chicken suit to school?

C Forget about being teased
and always remember
to treat others the way
you want to be treated?"

Pinky wished the answer was **A**.
She also thought **B**
was a great idea.
But she knew
the real answer
was **C**.

The next day,
Pinky hoped that
everyone had forgotten about
the little "toot."
But—no such luck.

"Stinky Pinky!

Stinky Pinky!"

Daffinee sang in gym class.

Everyone was laughing

and jumping around.

Pinky got really really mad.

She wanted to do something

to make Daffinee stop!

Then Pinky heard
a great big RRRRIIIPPP!
Daffinee had ripped out
the entire back of her dress.

And she was wearing underpants
with little bunny rabbits on them!

Daffinee looked at Pinky
with horror.
Pinky looked at Daffinee
and smiled.

Can you guess what
happened next?

Pinky Dinky Doo

decided to Think Big!

Normally,

Pinky had an average,

everyday,

kid-sized brain.

That is,

until she decided to think big.

Pinky thought

and thought.

There
she goes!

And as she thought,
her head got bigger and bigger
until she lifted off.

Wow. Pinky sure can think big!

And then . . .

33

Pinky had a big idea.

She could:

 Run Daffinee's bunny underpants
up a flagpole so everyone
would see them.

B Have a contest to see who could come up with the best new name for Daffinee.

DAFFINEE LAUGHINEE TOILETTE

MISS BUNNY BUTT!

MISS RRRRIIIPPP! VAN WINKLE

DAFF-I- NAH-NAH- NAH-NAH-NAH- NEE

C None of the above.

Of course.

The answer was **C**, of course.

Pinky decided to treat Daffinee
the way she wished Daffinee
had treated her.

Nobody would ever know that
Daffinee had ripped her dress or
that she had bunny underpants.

From that moment on,

things changed

for Daffinee and Pinky.

Daffinee didn't think Pinky

was just her friend.

Pinky was her best friend ever!

"And that's exactly
what happened . . .
sort of.

POOF!

The end,"
Pinky finished.

40

"Aw,"

said Tyler,

"that's it?"

"No!"

Pinky said.

"Every now and then,

Pinky would whisper to Daffinee,

'Hey,

Miss Bunny Butt!'

and Daffinee would reply,

'Hey yourself,

Miss Tooty Toot Toot!'

But they

NEVER

did it when anyone else was around.

The end."

"Woo-hoo,"

Tyler shouted.

"I loved that story,

Pinky."

"What did you like about it?"

Pinky asked.

"I liked Queen of the Toots,"

Tyler said,

"and President Stinky and—"

Pinky interrupted,

"What about what Daddy Doo said

about how you're supposed

to treat others?"

Tyler thought hard.

"Oh,

yeah,"

he said.

"So,"

said Pinky,

"how are you supposed

to treat others?"

Like I want them to treat ME?

"That's it,
little brother!"
Pinky handed Tyler
his clean socks.
"Okay,
Mr. Lucky Socks.
Put these on,
get out there,
and do it!"

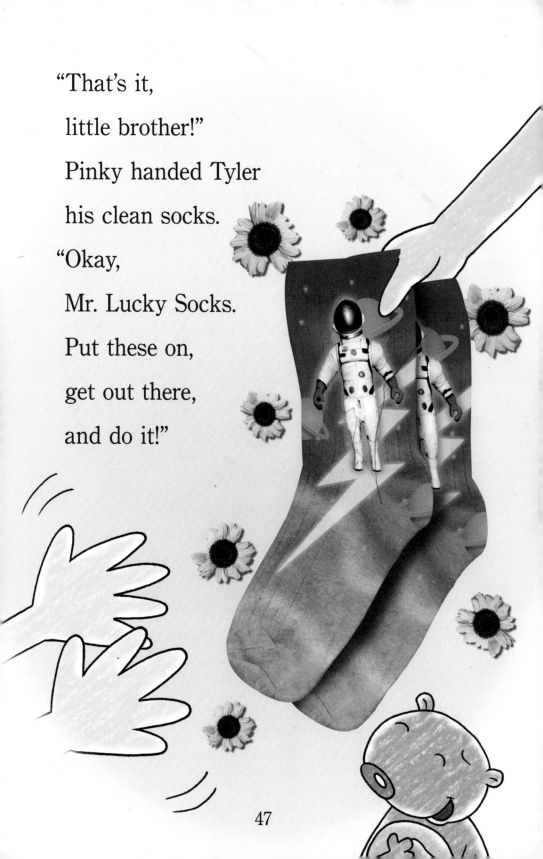

I hope you'll get out there and do it, too!